Piggybook

Anthony Browne

WALKER BOOKS
AND SUBSIDIARIES
LONDON • BOSTON • SYDNEY

First published in Great Britain 1986
by Julia MacRae Books

This edition published 1996
by Walker Books Ltd
87 Vauxhall Walk
London SE11 5HJ

10 9 8 7 6

Printed in Hong Kong

British Library Cataloguing in Publication Data
A catalogue record for this book is
available from the British Library.

ISBN 0-7445-3303-1

For Julia

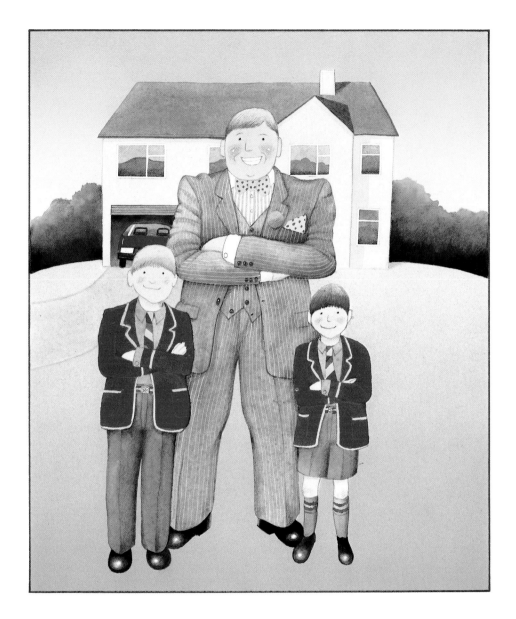

Mr Piggott lived with his two sons, Simon and Patrick, in a nice house with a nice garden, and a nice car in the nice garage.
Inside the house was his wife.

"Hurry up with the breakfast, dear," he called every morning,
before he went off to his very important job.

"Hurry up with the breakfast, Mum," Simon and Patrick called before they went off to their very important school.

After they left the house, Mrs Piggott washed all the breakfast things . . .

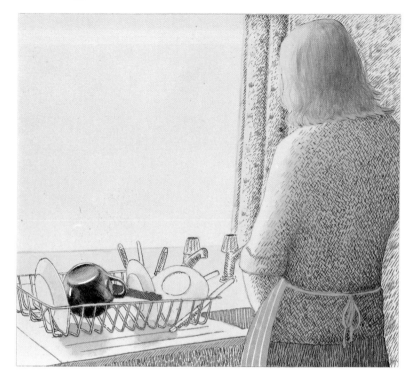

made all the beds . . .

vacuumed all the carpets . . .

and then she went to work.

"Hurry up with the meal, Mum," the boys called every evening when they came home from their very important school.

"Hurry up with the meal, old girl," Mr Piggott called every evening when he came home from his very important job.

As soon as they had eaten,
Mrs Piggott washed the dishes . . . washed the clothes . . .

did the ironing . . . and then she cooked some more.

One evening when the boys got home from school there was no-one to greet them.

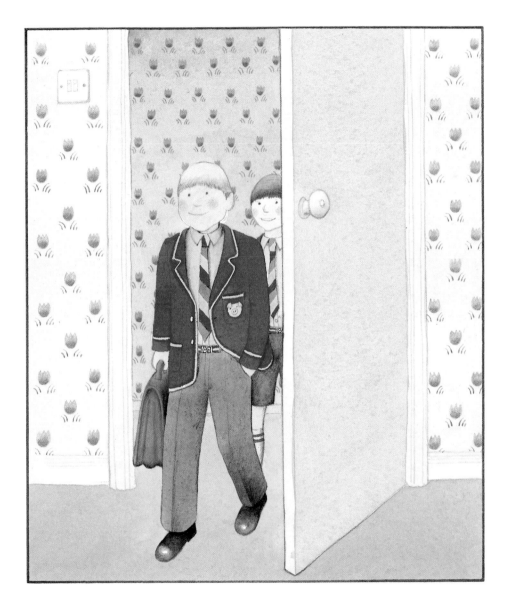

"Where's Mum?" demanded Mr Piggott when he got home from work.

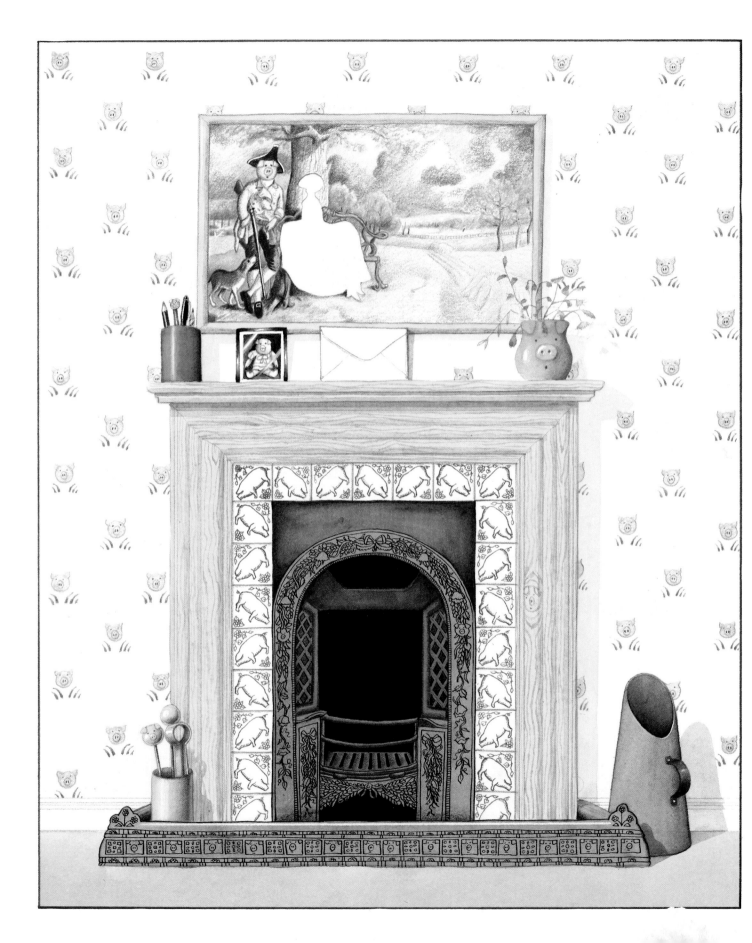

She was nowhere to be found.
On the mantelpiece was an envelope.
Mr Piggott opened it.
Inside was a piece of paper.

"But what shall we *do*?" said Mr Piggott.
They had to make their own meal.
It took hours.
And it was horrible.

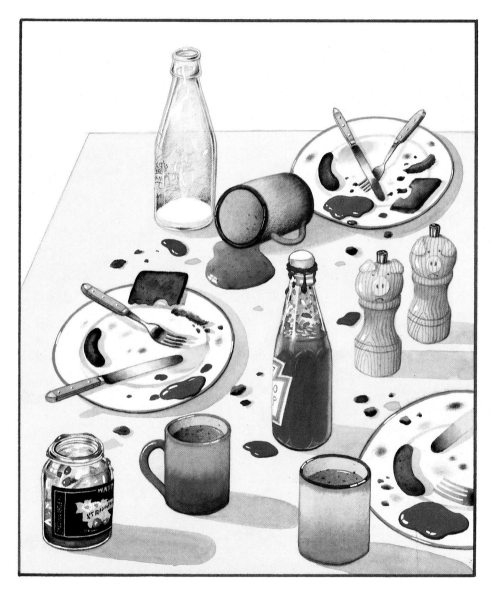

Next morning they had to make their
own breakfast.
It took hours.
And it was horrible.

The next day and the next night and the day after that, Mrs Piggott was still not there. Mr Piggott, Simon and Patrick tried to look after themselves.

They never washed the dishes. They never washed their clothes. Soon the house was like a pigsty.

"When is Mum coming home?" the boys squealed after another horrible meal.

"How should I know?" Mr Piggott grunted.

They all became more and more grumpy.

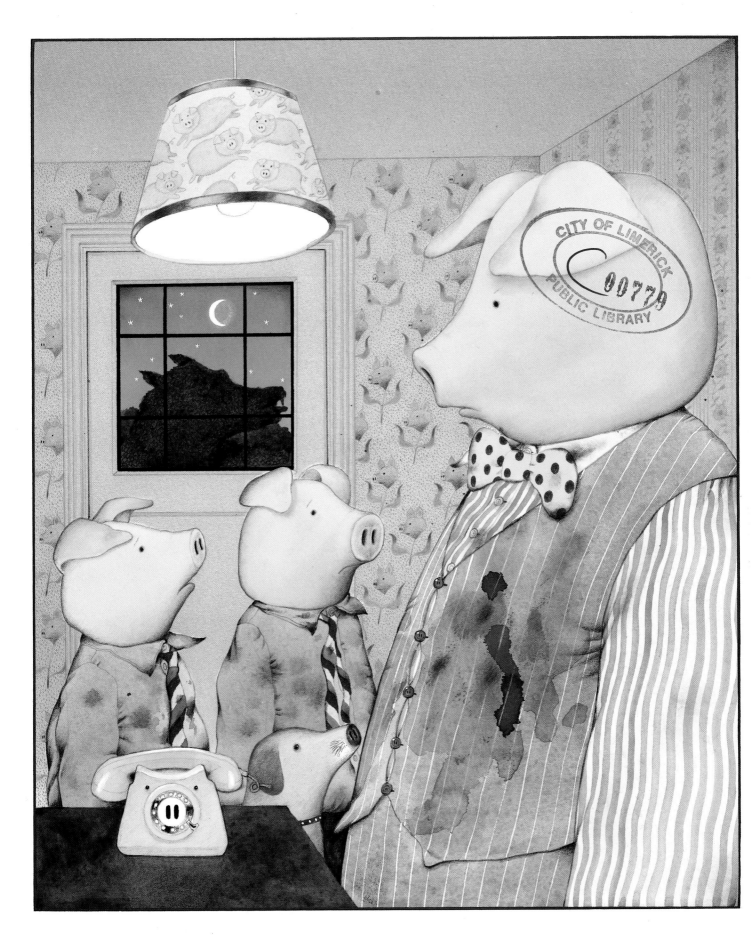

One night there was nothing in the house for them to cook.
"We'll just have to root around and find some scraps,"
snorted Mr Piggott.

And just then Mrs Piggott walked in.

Mum was happy too . . .

She mended the car.